R0110183555

04/201▌

P9-EIF-087

A Note to Parents

Welcome to REAL KIDS READERS, a series of phonics-based books for children who are beginning to read. In the classroom, educators use phonics to teach children how to sound out unfamiliar words, providing a firm foundation for reading skills. At home, you can use REAL KIDS READERS to reinforce and build on that foundation, because the books follow the same basic phonic guidelines that children learn in school.

Of course the best way to help your child become a good reader is to make the experience fun—and REAL KIDS READERS do that, too. With their realistic story lines and lively characters, the books engage children's imaginations. With their clean design and sparkling photographs, they provide picture clues that help new readers decipher the text. The combination is sure to entertain young children and make them truly want to read.

REAL KIDS READERS have been developed at three distinct levels to make it easy for children to read at their own pace.

- LEVEL 1 is for children who are just beginning to read.
- LEVEL 2 is for children who can read with help.
- LEVEL 3 is for children who can read on their own.

A controlled vocabulary provides the framework at each level. Repetition, rhyme, and humor help increase word skills. Because children can understand the words and follow the stories, they quickly develop confidence. They go back to each book again and again, increasing their proficiency and sense of accomplishment, until they're ready to move on to the next level. The result is a rich and rewarding experience that will help them develop a lifelong love of reading.

For my dad,
who likes old pants too
—M. L.

For my brothers, who always provided
the best hand-me-downs
—D. H.

Special thanks to Hanna Andersson, Portland, OR,
and to Lands' End, Dodgeville, WI, for providing clothing.

Produced by DWAI / Seventeenth Street Productions, Inc.
Reading Specialist: Virginia Grant Clammer

Millbrook Press
A division of Lerner Publishing Group, Inc.
241 First Avenue North
Minneapolis, MN 55401 USA

For reading levels and more information,
look up this title at www.lernerbooks.com.

Library of Congress Cataloging-in-Publication Data
Leonard, Marcia.
    No new pants! / Marcia Leonard ; photographs by Dorothy Handelman.
        p.   cm. — (Real kids readers. Level 1)
    Summary: When his mother takes him to buy new pants, a young boy tries on many
different pairs, but finds just what he wants back at home.
    ISBN 978–0–7613–2063–0 (lib. bdg. : alk. paper)
    ISBN 978–0–7613–2088–3 (pbk. : alk. paper)
    ISBN 978–0–7613–7375–9 (eb pdf)
    [1. Clothing and dress—Fiction. 2. Shopping—Fiction. 3. Mothers and sons—Fiction.
4. Stories in rhyme.] I. Handelman, Dorothy, ill. II. Title. III. Series.
PZ8.3.L54925No   1999
[E]—dc21   98-52514

Manufactured in the United States of America
8-43705-743-2/16/2017

No New Pants!

By Marcia Leonard

Photographs by Dorothy Handelman

ML Millbrook Press • Minneapolis

The sun is out.
I want to play.

5

But we have to shop today.

7

We shop for pants.
It is not fun.

I want to go.
I want to run.

I try on pants.
They are too small.

And these don't fit
my legs at all.

These pants are stiff.
These pants are hot.

I do not like these.
I do not!

We go back home.
My mom is mad.

I have a plan
to make her glad.

My brother's pants
are old and worn.

The legs are soft.
The knee is torn.

27

They are too small
for him, you see.

But they are just
the pants for me!

Reading with Your Child

1. Try to read with your child at least twenty minutes each day, as part of your regular routine.
2. Keep your child's books in one convenient, cozy reading spot.
3. Read and familiarize yourself with the Phonic Guidelines below.
4. Ask your child to read *No New Pants!* out loud. If he or she has difficulty with a word:
    • Help him or her decode the word phonetically. (Say, "Try to sound it out.")
    • Encourage him or her to use picture clues. (Say, "What does the picture show?")
    • Ask him or her to use context clues. (Say, "What would make sense?")
5. If your child still doesn't "get" the word, tell him or her what it is. Don't wait for frustration to build.
6. Praise your beginning reader. With your enthusiasm and encouragement, your child will go from one success to the next.

Phonic Guidelines

Use the following guidelines to help your child read the words in *No New Pants!*

Short Vowels
When two consonants surround a vowel, the sound of the vowel is usually short. This means you pronounce *a* as in apple, *e* as in egg, *i* as in igloo, *o* as in octopus, and *u* as in umbrella. Short-vowel words in this story include: *but, fit, fun, him, hot, legs, mad, mom, not, run, sun.*

Short-Vowel Words with Beginning Consonant Blends
When two different consonants begin a word, they usually blend to make a combined sound. Words in this story with beginning consonant blends include: *glad, plan, stiff.*

Short-Vowel Words with Ending Consonant Blends
When two different consonants end a word, they usually blend to make a combined sound. Words in this story with ending consonant blends include: *just, pants, soft.*

R-Controlled Vowels
When a vowel is followed by the letter *r*, its sound is changed by the *r*. Words in this story with r-controlled vowels are: *are, for, her, torn, worn.*

Double Consonants
When two identical consonants appear side by side, one of them is silent. In this story, double consonants appear in the *all*-family words *all* and *small.*

Sight Words
Sight words are those words that a reader must learn to recognize immediately—by sight—instead of by sounding them out. They occur with high frequency in easy texts. Sight words not included in the above categories are: *a, and, at, back, do, go, have, home, I, is, it, like, make, me, my, old, on, out, play, see, the, these, they, to, today, too, try, want, we, you.*